Marquis & Finds a Friend
© 2016 Mary J. Bryant
Kingdom Builders Publications, LLC

Any form or by any means without written permission from the author.

ISBN – 978-0-578-17290-3
Library of Congress Control Number – 2017940917

Printed in USA
Marilyn Dozier, Editor
Eric Quzack, Illustrator

Kingdom Builders Publications LLC

Dedicated

Our youngest son, Marquis (pronounced Markiss), took to dinosaurs very early. He never really played with other toys as much as he did with dinosaurs, so these series of books are dedicated to Marquis Jarod Bryant, now a man.

THIS IS MY BOOK

Marquis was a curious and creative little boy. He enjoyed playing outside and discovering new things. Marquis liked to walk along the path near his home. His Mother always sat on the porch to make sure he didn't wonder off too far. All the neighbors knew how adventurous Marquis was. So they also kept an eye out for Marquis.

One day while Marquis was walking down the road chasing butterflies, he heard sounds of someone crying. He peeked over the bushes and could not believe his eyes. He saw a little dinosaur sitting on the ground. The little dinosaur was crying because he was lost.

Marquis cautiously approached him. "Hi, my name is Marquis." What is your name and why are you crying?" asked Marquis. Wiping the tears from his eyes, the scared little dinosaur replied, "My name is Sebastian. I am lost and cannot find my Mother."

Sebastian was lost because as he and his Mother were on a picnic together, he decided to wander away by himself. He loved his Mother and wanted to surprise her with some flowers. So he sneaked away without letting her know that he was going.

Sebastian knew his Mother would not let him go off by himself. As he walked through the forest trying to find the perfect flowers, he suddenly saw the most beautiful flowers he had ever seen! Sebastian was so excited that he hurried over to pick them. Once he had picked all the flowers he could carry, he started back to the picnic area.

As Sebastian skipped along, he realized that he was going around in circles. He started to become scared as he ran through the forest calling for his Mother. "Mother, Mother!" yelled the frightened little dinosaur. He searched and searched, but he could not find his way back. He was tired and very scared. He began to cry as he sat under a nearby bush.

Once Marquis found out that Sebastian was lost he felt very sad for him. Marquis touched his shoulder and said, "I will help you find your Mother. Don't be afraid."

Marquis made the little lost dinosaur very happy. He wiped his face and sprang to his feet. The two of them started out to find Sebastian's Mother. Marquis and Sebastian looked and looked. They searched everywhere but could not find his Mother.

Hours passed and it started to get dark. Marquis' Mother began to call for him to come back home. "Boo—ooh!" cried Sebastian "I want my Mother." Marquis was sad for Sebastian and couldn't leave him out in the forest alone. He put his hand on his shoulder again, "Don't worry Sebastian.", Marquis said, "We will find your Mother."

"But it is getting too dark to be out here in the forest. You can come home with me for the night and we will start back looking for your Mother in the morning." Little Sebastian was so tired and hungry he agreed to go with Marquis. So off they went to Marquis' house.

Marquis' Mother was shocked when she saw Marquis walking back with a little dinosaur at his side. "Marquis, who do we have here?" She asked. "This is Sebastian." Marquis replied. "He is lost and can't find his Mother." Marquis put his arm around him to make him feel at ease.

Feeling sad for the little dinosaur, Marquis' Mother gently patted Sebastian's head to help him feel safe. "It is okay; you may stay here tonight and tomorrow Marquis and I will help you find your Mother." He nodded his head with a smile on his face. Of course, Marquis' Mother had to pat Marquis' head as well.

"Are you hungry?" asked Marquis' Mother.
"Yes", nodded Sebastian. So the two of them
went and washed their hands for dinner.
They had spaghetti and meatballs for
dinner. Marquis and his Mother was shocked
when Sebastian slurped up the last of
Marquis' spaghetti too. He was quite
hungry.

That night after the two of them went to bed, Marquis' Mother heard Sebastian crying. She went into the room to find out what was wrong. Marquis told his Mother that Sebastian was home sick for his Mother. Marquis' Mother sang him a lullaby to help him fall sleep. Before long both Marquis and Sebastian were fast asleep.

The next day Marquis reaches over to wake up Sebastian. The two of them hurried downstairs to find Marquis' Mother. She was in the kitchen making them breakfast. Once they finished their breakfast, Marquis and his Mother went with Sebastian to help him find his Mother.

Marquis, was so excited that his Mother was going with them to look for Sebastian's Mother. Marquis was skipping and jumping as they walked along the path. "Sebastian, does any of this look familiar too you?" Marquis' asked. Looking around, Sebastian shook his head "No". Marquis' Mother reassured him that they would find his mother today. "Yes, my Mother will help you find your Mother." Marquis exclaimed.

After looking for the Mother for a long time, Marquis decided to run ahead of everyone. As he was chasing a butterfly, he looked up and there was Sebastian's Mother coming towards them. She was trying to find him also. Marquis was so excited that they had found his new friend's Mother.

"Sebastian!" Marquis yelled. "Look, it is your Mother!"

Sebastian was so excited to finally see his Mother. "Mother! Mother!" yelled Sebastian as he ran as fast as he could towards her. "I am so glad to see you!" She opened her arms and in he ran. She hugged and kissed him with great joy. "Where have you been Sebastian? I have been so worried about you." Sebastian's Mother exclaimed.

With his head held down, Sebastian explained that he wanted to surprise her with some flowers but he got lost. That is when Marquis found me and took me to his house. This is Marquis and his Mother. Everyone said hello to each other. Sebastian's Mother thanked Marquis and his Mother for taking care of her son and helping him find his way back to her.

Then the Mother dinosaur said in a stern caring voice, "Don't ever wander away from me without permission again. It is too dangerous for you to go off by yourself." Sebastian looked down once again at his feet and said, "Yes, Mother. I will not wander away again."

Marquis found a new friend and Sebastian was so happy he found his Mother. Marquis said, "Children should not sneak away from their parents without permission." Sebastian learned a valuable lesson and he never wandered away from his Mother again.

About the Author

Mary J. Bryant is an inspirational and children's author. Her love for children, moral living inspired her first children's book, Marquis Finds a Friend, which begins Marquis and his adventures series. Mary is married with three children and granddaughter. This book was inspired by their youngest son, Marquis. Dinosaurs were his favorite past time entertainment as a child. He wandered from his mother as was Sebastian in this story.